LATKE, THE LUCKY DOG

ELLEN FISCHER   illustrations by **TIPHANIE BEEKE**

KAR-BEN
PUBLISHING

Dedicated with love to Jazzie and Maggie —E.F.

For Robert and Alex, Happy Hanukkah, with love —T.B.

Text copyright © 2014 by Ellen Fischer
Illustrations copyright © 2014 by Lerner Publishing Group, Inc.

Kar-Ben Publishing
A division of Lerner Publishing Group, Inc.
241 First Avenue North
Minneapolis, MN 55401 USA
1-800-4-KARBEN

Website address: www.karben.com

Main body text set in EatwellSkinny.
Typeface provided by Chank.

Library of Congress Cataloging-in-Publication Data

Fischer, Ellen, 1947–
    Latke, the lucky dog / by Ellen Fischer ; illustrated by Tiphanie Beeke.
    Summary: "A family rescues a dog from a shelter during Hanukkah, and
the pup proceeds to create holiday hijinks as he gets used to his new home"—
Provided by publisher.
       pages   cm.
    ISBN 978–0–7613–9038–1 (lib. bdg. : alk. paper)
    [1. Dogs—Fiction. 2. Hanukkah—Fiction.] I. Beeke, Tiphanie, illustrator. II. Title.
PZ7.F498766Lat 2014
[E]—dc23   2013022212

Manufactured in the United States of America
1 – BP – 7/15/2014

I am one lucky dog! Imagine a mutt like me picked as a Hanukkah present.

It happened one day in December when a family walked into the shelter. A mom, a dad and two kids—Zoe and Zach.

Zach said, "I want a big dog."

Uh-oh, I thought. I'm not big.

But Zoe said, "I want a little dog that'll fit in my doll stroller."

I tried to curl up as small as possible, but I'm not little.

Then Mom said, "Let's compromise and look for a medium-sized dog."

Yep! That's me. I danced around and wagged my tail. Finally they noticed me.

Dad said, "Look at this one. He's playful, medium-sized, and golden brown, like a fried latke."

And that's how it happened. They took me home on the first
night of Hanukkah and named me Latke. I am one lucky dog!

As we came into the kitchen, something smelled delicious.

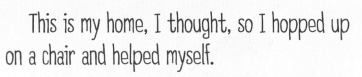

This is my home, I thought, so I hopped up
on a chair and helped myself.

But Zoe said, "Latke ate all the sufganiyot!"

Then Zach patted me on the head and said, "Poor, hungry Latke. They didn't feed you enough at that shelter, did they?"

Thanks, Zach.

I am one lucky dog!

On the second night of Hanukkah, boxes wrapped in paper and bows were on the floor.

I'm the new guy, so they must be for me, I figured. I tore them open, but there was nothing for a dog.

Look what Latke did," said Zach. "He tore our presents."

Time for me to hide behind a chair.

But Zoe picked me up and said, "You were just trying to help, weren't you, cutie pie? We'll wrap them back up and pretend nothing happened."

Thanks, Zoe.
I am one lucky dog.

On the third night, I smelled something frying.

"Now don't touch these," Mom said, shaking her finger at me.

"Latkes!" shouted Zoe.

Dinner for me? So I ate them all.

"Bad dog!" said Mom.

"You heard your name, didn't you boy?" said Zach. "We can still have Hanukkah without latkes."

Whew!
I am one lucky dog.

On the fourth night, I tried to spin Zoe's dreidel, but it got chewed up.

Zoe said, "Oh, no, Latke, that was my favorite one."

Uh-oh. This time she didn't call me cutie pie.

Zoe, Zach, and I played chase on the fifth night. Oops! We knocked over the bowl of applesauce.

Time to hide behind the chair again.

On the sixth night, I saw something shiny on the floor next to the dreidels.

I'm not chewing those dreidels again, I thought, but I take a few sniffs and licks to investigate.

Zoe ran to dad. "Latke slobbered all over the chocolate Hanukkah gelt."

"Maybe we picked the wrong dog," said Dad.

No, no! I'm the right dog. I love it here. I just need to learn the rules.

On the seventh night, I found colored sticks on the table. Chew toys maybe? But they get stuck in my teeth. Yuck!

"Look," cried Zoe. "Latke chewed all the candles. Now we can't light the menorah. This time Hanukkah is really ruined."

But Zach took the waxy mess out of my mouth. A little dog slobber didn't bother him.

"We can use our other menorah with the wicks and oil, just like the Maccabees did," he said.

I think I get it now. I eat just what's in my dog dish. But I hope it's not too late.

On the last night of Hanukkah I tried extra hard to be good. Before dinner my family gave me a present.

"Here, Latke, you cutie pie, this is for you. Open it," said Zoe.

"Rip off the paper," said Zach.

No way. I just sat there like the perfect pet. I don't want to go back to the shelter. Finally, they opened it for me.

"It's a chew toy, for our own Latke. You can chew this all you want," said Zoe.

For me? My very own chew toy? What a great family I have!

I am one lucky dog!

ABOUT HANUKKAH

Hanukkah is an eight-day Festival of Lights that celebrates the victory of the Maccabees over the mighty armies of the Syrian King Antiochus. According to legend, when the Maccabees came to restore the Holy Temple in Jerusalem, they found one jug of pure oil, enough to keep the menorah lit for just one day. But a miracle happened, and the oil burned for eight days. On each night of the holiday, we add an additional candle to the menorah, exchange gifts, play the game of dreidel, and eat latkes and *sufganiyot* (jelly donuts), which are fried in oil, to remember this victory for religious freedom.

ELLEN FISCHER was born in St. Louis. A graduate of Washington University, she has taught children with special needs and ESL (English as a Second Language) at a Jewish Day School. She lives in Greensboro, North Carolina. Her previous books include the Shalom Sesame® titles *The Count's Hanukkah Countdown; I'm Sorry, Grover!; Grover and Big Bird's Passover Celebration;* and *It's a Mitzvah, Grover.*

TIPHANIE BEEKE is the illustrator of many children's books. She lives in the south of France with her husband, three children, two cats, and a goldfish. She enjoys eating outside and wearing perfume. Her favorite things to draw are foxes and dogs so she was delighted to illustrate *Latke, the Lucky Dog!*